5.95

W9-AEU-448

play little victims

play little victims

Kenneth Cook

illustrated by Megan Gressor

Pergamon Press

Pergamon Press (Australia) Pty Limited,
19a Boundary Street, Rushcutters Bay, NSW 2011

A. Wheaton & Company, A Division of Pergamon Press,
Hennock Road, Exeter, EX2 8RP

Pergamon Press Ltd, Headington Hill Hall, Oxford OX3 0BW

Pergamon Press Inc, Maxwell House,
Fairview Park, Elmsford, New York 10523

Pergamon of Canada Ltd,
75 The East Mall, Toronto, Ontario M8Z 2L9, Canada

Pergamon Press GmbH, 6242 Kronberg/Taunus,
Pferdstrasse 1, Frankfurt-am-Main, West Germany

Pergamon Press SARL,
24 rue des Ecoles, 75240 Paris, Cedex 05, France

Cover design by Allan Hondow
Typeset in Brisbane by Savage & Co.
Printed in Singapore by Singapore National Printers

National Library of Australia
Cataloguing in Publication data
Cook, Kenneth, 1929–
    Play little victims.
    ISBN 0 08 023123 3
    I. Title.
A823.3

Play little victims

Alas, regardless of their doom,
The little victims play!
No sense have they of ills to come,
Nor cares beyond today.

THOMAS GRAY

1

Life on earth was eliminated in the year 2000.

This, of course, was the end of the second millenium. God was supposed to have done something about it at the end of the first millenium, but He had forgotten, so at the end of the second millenium He thought He'd better take some definitive action.

He contemplated His handiwork for a split fraction of Infinity, then said, "Oh God!" or words to that effect.

"There's absolutely nothing to be done with a mess like that," He muttered to Himself, so He decided there and then to eliminate the place. It was not possible to make it disappear altogether, because

1

that would have caused enormous complications in the rest of the universe, so He crooked His little finger and caused all life on earth to vanish, painlessly and permanently. Then He crooked it again and wrapped the earth in a vast layer of ice, many hundreds of metres thick. Finally He crooked His finger a third time and caused a vast, thick white cloud to envelop the earth, so that it wasn't possible for any other being in the universe to see what had happened. He did this because He was a little worried about the theological implications of His actions, and didn't want to get involved in interminable arguments with His company of saints.

Satisfied that that was the end of that, God went and rested.

2

However, God had blundered.

To understand how, it is necessary to know that the wriggle of God's finger was only the initial motivation in an extremely complex re-arrangement of physical laws. These involved gravity, the ionosphere, Newton's law, an enormous number of Euclidean propositions, the theory of evolution, and the science of genetics.

Because He was just a little too anxious to forget the whole thing, He didn't quite pull off the job as efficiently as He would have done in the days when He spent His time counting the hairs on men's heads and watching sparrows fall.

3

Without going into too much technical detail, what happened was that an area of a few square kilometres surrounded by some high mountains, roughly in the centre of the United States, had not received the full effect of God's finger wriggling. The whole valley had escaped the ice-cap and a pair of fieldmice, deep in a hole in the ground, had failed to vanish.

In themselves these two exceptions to God's intentions would not have mattered, but there was more to it than that. The cosmic convulsion had completely disrupted the theory of evolution, obviously because God felt there would be no further use for it. But the mice, on the tag-end of the theory as far as time was concerned, found, to their considerable surprise, that they had advanced by several million years. They could think and they could talk, as men had thought and talked.

"Goodness," said the mice to each other. "We can think, therefore we are." Which was a considerable advance on anything any mouse had produced before.

The mice were only young and had just set up house together. Of course in the past they had only been mindless little creatures unconsciously following the Divine Plan. Even now, despite their acute intelligence, they had no idea what they were or where they came from.

Cautiously, paw in paw, they crept out of their hole, and looked around at the world for the first time with intelligent eyes. All they could see from the top of the hole was a few blades of grass, a stone and the base of a tree.

"Well, what do you think of that?" said the male mouse. "Look, a few blades of grass, a stone and the base of a tree."

"There's got to be more to it than that," said the

female mouse. "Incidentally, what's your name?"

"My name?" said the male mouse. "My name? Oh yes. I must have a name." Reaching deep into what must have been a grossly miscegenated race memory he said, "I think my name is Adamus."

"Quite," said the female mouse. "And I'm Evemus."

"Good, then that's settled," said Adamus. "Let's go and see what we can find."

They found that they were the only animals in the valley, which didn't surprise them because they didn't know that there had ever been such things as other animals. They also found a town, quite empty of life, but complete with lots of houses, two schools, a library, a television station, three radio stations, an automobile factory, a newspaper, a police station, a fire station, an ambulance station and all the paraphenalia that you would expect to find in a prosperous town in the middle of the United States.

From the tip of the mast of the television station they surveyed the valley. It was bounded by great walls of ice on top of the mountains, which formed the limits of the world as far as they were concerned. It was a fertile valley, well planted with crops and fruit trees. There wasn't much sunlight because of the cloud layers God had wrapped around the earth, but mice are nocturnal creatures anyway so they didn't mind the dimness. All in all, Adamus and Evemus felt they had everything a mouse could desire.

"Well, what do we do now?" said Adamus.

"We move out of that hole we've been living in and move into one of those houses," said Evemus promptly.

They chose the most imposing house, a white mansion built on the highest point in the town, and moved in. Everything in the house was a bit big for them, but they contrived to make themselves very comfortable nonetheless, and after some experimenting managed to open the refrigerator and prepare themselves an excellent supper.

"You know," said Adamus, sitting on the verandah that evening, watching the extraordinary effects created on the cloud layer by the sun setting below the ice-rim, "all this wasn't meant for just you and me, Evemus."

"No," Evemus replied, "I was just thinking that myself."

"I mean, there's enough here for a million mice."

"More," said Evemus.

"So what do you think?"

"I think," said Evemus, "that we had better be fruitful and multiply."

6

3

An ordinary, irrational pair of mice, without putting their minds to it, could breed at a tremendous rate in the old days. Adamus and Evemus, rational, dedicated to their task and untroubled by the vicissitudes that used previously to plague mice, performed wonders. Their first litter, ten superb specimens, appeared three weeks after the Beginning, as they came to term their acquisition of rationality. Within another three weeks all these mice were busily engaged in procreating, so that nine weeks after the Beginning there were several hundred mice in the Valley. Nine weeks after that there were so many mice that it became necessary to take a census,

9

and the population was found to stand at 1,562. But it didn't stand at that for very long—about five minutes in fact.

As every mouse descended from Adamus and Evemus possessed the blessing of intelligence, it was no time at all before they had grasped all the technicalities of the town that had been so inexplicably bequeathed to them. By the time the population reached 3,000 they had everything working well and indeed, with the obvious adaptations necessary because of their size, managed to reproduce a mouse lifestyle virtually identical to the lifestyle enjoyed by the human beings who had inhabited the town before the Beginning.

Naturally Adamus became the leader, and Evemus his respected consort. They continued to live in the white mansion on the hill and watched contentedly as their descendants created for themselves an extremely pleasant place in which to work out their destinies.

Adamus became a great scholar. Because everything was so exciting and new and everybody was so busy and happy, the job of leader was very much a sinecure and Adamus spent most of his time in the town library, rummaging through the files of the newspaper office, and studying films that he had discovered in the television station. It was from these sources, Adamus felt, that he could learn the origin of his being.

Most of this material he found completely baffling, but he persisted and read right through the works of Shakespeare, Bertrand Russell, Mickey Spillane, Georgette Heyer, Freud, Graham Greene and Neta Muskett, as well as the Bible, 4,628 editions of the New York Times, and just about everything else he could lay his paws on. Very soon he became a highly, if haphazardly,

10

educated mouse.

On the day the population in the Valley reached 5,000 Adamus decided to broadcast over all three radio stations, in order to give the community the benefits of his research.

"Fellow mice," he said. "No doubt you have all been wondering, as I have been wondering, just who we are, where we came from, and why we are here."

Most of the mice had been too busy making themselves comfortable to wonder any such thing, but they all looked solemn and pretended they had been thinking of little else.

"I mean," continued Adamus, "it is obvious to all that this wonderful world in which we live did not just happen by accident. There has to be a Divine Plan and we are part of that Plan. We have a destiny which we must fulfil."

The mice all looked at each other and nodded wisely.

"Well," said Adamus, "I have discovered what it's all about. What happened was this: the source of all being is God, who made the Valley and everything else in the universe. To prepare the way for mousekind God sent a sort of vanguard of creatures he called Men, who might best be thought of as sort of supermice. These Men prepared the Valley for us and left us all these marvellous technological aids for our existence. They also left us a vast body of literature for our guidance. Our destiny in life is to fulfil the plan of God by making the Valley an extension of Heaven. To guide us in this task we have the Word of Man, so we just can't go wrong."

The more Adamus talked the more he found his theory made sense. If he had been perfectly honest with himself he would have admitted that when he began his broadcast he felt there were a few holes in his thesis, but as he propounded it over the airwaves he became convinced that he was dead right.

"Now obviously," he continued, "the interpretation of the Word of Man is a matter of some importance to us. As I have already begun the task, I suggest I continue and set up a School of Homological Studies for the permanent guidance of the race of mice. In the meantime I would like to impress upon you the first and most important dictum which Man has left for our guidance. That is "God is Love". That is the rule by which Man lived, as far as I can make out, and that is the rule by which we should live. Thank you all and good-night."

All that was probably as good as any prophet would have done, working from the position in which Adamus found himself, but neither he nor his fellow mice really understood the nature of God or of Love, which is hardly surprising.

However, they applied themselves to living by this first dictum of Man as best they could, with the result that three weeks later the population of the Valley stood at just on eight thousand mice.

With the increase in population it became obvious that the mice of the Valley needed a formal governing body. Adamus set out to discover what the Word of Man was on the subject, and made a valiant attempt to analyse the United States electoral system. Deciding, in his humility, that he was not yet sufficiently learned to understand Man's method of government, he finally set out a plan for a sort of interim Board to control the Valley. Each member of this Board had a certain field of responsibility and took his general guidelines from the Word of Man, as handed down by Adamus. The Board consisted of a member for Science, Education and Related Subjects, known as Sciemus; a member for Radio, Television and Newspapers, known as Mediamus; a member for Food and Water Supplies, known as Fawsmus; and a member for Matters of General Interest (which covered everything the other three didn't), who was known as Mogimus. Adamus was Chairmouse of the Board and had power to appoint other members if and as required.

13

By now Adamus had his School of Homological Studies well established, and a learned body of ten mice was constantly combing through the human records left in the Valley to discover the Word of Man as it applied to the various problems the mice encountered on their road to perfection. Because of the pressure of his duties Adamus appointed an assistant, who became, in effect, Head of the School of Homological Studies. This mouse was known as Logimus and had the right to sit on the Board, but only in an advisory capacity.

The Board functioned well in handling the problems of the Valley, because at this stage there just weren't any. The mice had all they needed to make themselves very comfortable indeed. It was true that the number of mice greatly exceeded the number of human beings who had previously inhabited the Valley, but they were much smaller and soon realised that a house that had once accommodated three or four human beings made excellent high-rise accommodation for several thousand mice. The grain-fields and orchards provided them with more than enough food, and by way of raw materials for their rapidly developing industries they had the supplies left by their human predecessors which, because everything the mice manufactured was so small, seemed to be enough to last for thousands of years.

So the mice worked contentedly by day, and by night devoted themselves religiously to the study of the first dictum of Man, and watching television.

And there was peace in the Valley and goodwill among mice.

Until Logimus discovered mathematics.

4

Logimus came into the Board Meeting clutching a sheaf of papers covered with calculations. He plumped them down on the table and sat with a brooding expression on his intelligent little face, while the Board members presented their weekly reports to the Chairmouse. Usually Logimus had some useful or other comment to make on the reports, but today he didn't even seem to be listening to them. Adamus, who had come to rely on Logimus' analysis of the reports, glanced at him irritably, and twice coughed expectantly in his direction, but Logimus sat hunched over his papers in silence, fiddling all the time with a slide-rule, as though checking his figures.

Finally all the reports were read and Adamus called for any other business items. Logimus waited until it was obvious that no-one else had any other business, then gravely rose to his feet.

"Mr Chairmouse," he said, "gentlemice: I wish to bring to your attention a matter of grave import."

The Board members settled comfortably in their chairs. Administering the Valley had been so easy so far that it gave them quite a thrill to discover they had something of grave import to deal with.

Logimus shuffled his papers and paused until he was sure every member of the Board was paying attention.

"It is now," said Logimus, "just twelve months from the Beginning, and the population of the Valley stands at eleven thousand mice."

The Board all nodded intelligently.

"Now each of these mice is the descendant of our beloved Chairmouse and his good lady."

The Board automatically turned and bowed its heads in deference to the Chairmouse, who smiled deprecatingly.

"In other words gentlemice, Mr Chairmouse, in the Beginning there were two mice, and now, one year later, there are eleven thousand."

The Board members shuffled in their seats. This was all a bit elementary. Was Logimus about to propose some sort of celebratory function? If so, it would be better if he came to the point.

"Now," continued Logimus in his slow, precise manner, "the area of the Valley is just on sixty square kilometres. At the perimeter of the Valley lies the Ice Barrier, beyond which no mouse can live."

The Board began to cough and twitch its whiskers. Really, if all Logimus intended was to give a speech on natural history it was too bad of him. The Board was conscious that it was nearly lunch-time.

"Sixty square kilometres is plenty of room for eleven thousand mice," continued Logimus. "It is enough to live in comfortably and provide us with all that we might reasonably require."

"Hear, hear," interjected Sciemus dryly, hoping that a little sarcasm might bring Logimus to the point.

"However," said Logimus, ignoring Sciemus, "has it occurred to any of you that each of us, each of the eleven thousand mice now living, carries within himself the same capacities for procreation as the Chairmouse and his lady?"

The Board exchanged glances, wondering whether Logimus was being disrespectful, or worse, slightly indelicate.

18

"In other words," said Logimus, "if starting from two mice at the Beginning there are now eleven thousand mice, one year later, how many mice will there be one year from now?"

"Conundrums before lunch yet," murmured Sciemus to Mogimus.

"This is not a conundrum, Sciemus," said Logimus severely. "It is an example of the exponential law of growth and decay. Do any of you have any idea how many mice will be in this Valley one year from now, at the present rate of increase?"

Realising that Logimus was genuinely trying to bring their attention to what he considered to be a matter of grave import, the Board tried to answer his question.

"Fifty-eight thousand?" said Sciemus, after thinking for a moment and doing some surreptitious counting on his fingers.

19

"One million," said Mogimus.

Mediamus and Fawsmus shook their heads, mutely admitting that the calculation was beyond them.

"Mr Chairmouse?" said Logimus.

Adamus knitted his brow.

"Well," he said, "I see that it has to be quite a large number—perhaps two million?"

Logimus looked long and steadily at the Board, who were all beginning to feel that they had a headache on the way.

"In one year from now," said Logimus slowly and carefully, "there will be sixty million mice living in the Valley."

"Sixty?" said Adamus.

"Million?" said Sciemus.

"Sixty million?" said Mediamus.

"Sixty?" said Mogimus.

"Million?" said Fawsmus.

"Sixty million mice," said Logimus firmly. "At least."

There was a long silence, as each member of the Board tried to encompass the enormous figure in his own tiny brain.

"Are you sure that's right?" said Sciemus finally, weakly.

"Obviously," said Logimus, "the rate at which the population grows is proportional to the population in the first place."

"Obviously," muttered Sciemus doubtfully.

"In this case the population in the first place is eleven thousand."

"Yes. We've grasped that," said Sciemus testily.

"So in a year's time the population will equal eleven

thousand times the exponential constant raised to the power of the constant times the time."

"Will it?" squeaked Sciemus.

"It will," said Logimus sternly.

"And that figure is . . ."

"Sixty million," said Logimus. "At least."

There was another long pause.

"Well," said Adamus, who had been thinking hard. "Is that bad?"

Logimus gave a deep sigh.

"Mr Chairmouse. We have sixty square kilometres in which to exist. Do you know how many square metres there are in sixty square kilometres?"

"Not offhand," said Adamus, a little huffily.

"Well it's sixty million."

"Sixty million," said Sciemus. "That seems a nice lot."

"A nice lot?" said Logimus. "There will be about one square metre of Valley space per mouse."

The Board sat back in its chairs and smiled.

"Well Logimus," said Adamus, "what are you pulling such a long face for?"

"Quite," said Sciemus. "One square metre might not be what we're used to, but we'll get by."

The others all nodded comfortably.

"And what about one year after that?" said Logimus.

"One year after that?" said Adamus slowly, as the implication became clear to him.

"One year after that," said Logimus inexorably. "Well, within the lifetime of every mouse alive today, there will be several million mice on every square metre of the Valley."

21

The Board gaped.

"One year after that," Logimus continued, "there will be a solid mass of mice jam-packed to the Ice Barrier on every side, and rising five kilometres into the air."

"Five kilometres?" said Sciemus.

"Into the air?" said Mogimus.

"But that's impossible," said Adamus.

"Of course it is," said Logimus, "and it won't happen."

The Board relaxed.

"It won't happen," said Sciemus. "Of course not. Why not?"

"Because long before we reach that point every mouse in the Valley will have died."

"Died?" said Adamus. "What of?"

"Died of the fact that it's impossible to be part of a five-kilometre-high mass of mice; died of starvation; died of pestilence; died of being crushed; died of heartbreak at the sheer impossibility of living in an impossible situation."

"Goodness," said Adamus, impressed at the fervour with which Logimus spoke. "Goodness. Is there nothing we can do about it?"

"Perhaps we had better convene a committee to look into it," said Sciemus.

"That's a good idea," said everybody else, except Logimus.

"Gentlemice," said Logimus. "There will never be anything in your lives as important as this. I suggest you devote your full energies to coming up with a solution as soon as possible."

Adamus stood up.

"Gentlemice," he said. "We should be grateful to

Logimus for bringing this problem so vividly to our notice. It is obviously a great problem and one we must solve. However, as I said in my inaugural address, the function of mousekind in the Valley is to work out the Divine Plan according to the Word of Man. This problem in itself is part of this Plan, as the solution will be. It simply behoves us to find that solution, which we shall do by consulting the Word of Man. Which of course we shall do promptly."

"Of course," said everybody, except Logimus, who was looking very thoughtful.

"I shall personally devote the next week to studying the problem with the aid of the staff of the School of Homological Studies, and will then report back to you," Adamus finished.

As the Board members went home for lunch they were uneasily aware of how many more mice there seemed to be on the streets than there had been a month or so before.

5

"As I suspected, the answer is quite simple," said Adamus complacently, at the Special Board Meeting on Population Control.

The five whiskered faces around the table looked at him expectantly.

"The problem is not that there are too many mice, but that mice live too long."

"What do you propose doing about that?" interjected Logimus. "Advocating mass suicide?"

Adamus looked at him witheringly.

"Suicide is wrong," he said. "It is against the Word of Man. But Man, too, faced this problem of overpopulation."

"He did?" said Sciemus.

"Not quite to the same extent that we do," conceded Adamus, "because Man's world seems to have been much larger than ours, but the problem was exactly the same in kind—it differed only in degree."

"And he had a solution?" asked Sciemus.

"He did," said Adamus triumphantly. "War."

"War?" said the Board.

"War," said Adamus.

"But wouldn't that be dangerous?" asked Logimus.

"Not at all. It provides a lot of healthy exercise, creates employment, boosts the economy, and, if enthusiastically pursued, eliminates the population problem."

"But wouldn't a lot of mice get killed?" pursued Logimus.

"Of course. That's the point," said Adamus. "As the population grows we have bigger and better wars to keep it in check."

"But surely it is against the Word of Man to kill?" said Logimus.

"Not at all, if the cause is just," said Adamus. "Man was always doing it, so it must be right."

"And Man conducted wars as a means of population control?"

"I'm certain of it," said Adamus. "There was no other possible reason for them."

The Board was looking worried, and it was Sciemus who put its concern into words.

"Would we have to take part in these wars?" he asked.

"Who?" said Adamus. "Us? The Board?"

"Yes," said Sciemus.

"No," said Adamus definitely. "The Board of a State does not take part in wars; it organises them. That is its proper function."

The Board relaxed and looked less worried.

"Who will the war be between?" asked Mogimus.

"Between the right-handed mice and the left-handed mice," said Adamus, who'd obviously already given this a great deal of thought.

"That was the way Men did it?" asked Sciemus.

"At the End, just before the Beginning," said Adamus authoritatively, "when Man was at his greatest peak of perfection, ready to hand the world over to us, he was occupying himself almost exclusively with battles of one sort or another between the Right and the Left."

"And that meant their hands?" asked Logimus doubtfully.

"There was nothing else to distinguish between the two groups," said Adamus, "so it must have been. Why not? It's as good a reason for taking sides as any put up by Man."

"All right then," said Sciemus. "Let's have a war." The three other members of the Board clapped and thumped the table with their paws. Only Logimus remained unmoved.

"Mr Chairmouse," he said respectfully. Adamus sat down and graciously indicated that Logimus had the floor.

"I wonder if we have not got the wrong end of the problem," said Logimus. "Surely instead of talking about population control we should be considering copulation control."

There was a shocked silence in the Boardroom.

"Copulation control?" said Adamus at last, not at all

sure that he had heard correctly.

"Yes," said Logimus. "No copulating, no populating. It's quite simple. You could even make quite a good slogan out of it," he added, unaware of the shock on the faces of the Board.

"No copulating?" said Adamus, his voice hushed.

"No populating," said Logimus brightly. "Catchy, eh?"

Adamus rose to his full nine centimetres.

"Sit down Logimus!" he thundered.

"Eh?" said Logimus, surprised at the rage which suffused Adamus's little furry face, so that the whiskers positively tangled.

"Sit down," roared Adamus, or he thought he was roaring. It was more of a high pitched squeal.

Abashed, Logimus sat down.

"What did I do wrong?" he muttered.

"The first law of Man," said Adamus, "is that God is Love."

"Yes," said Logimus, "but do you think that necessarily means ..."

"Of course it does," shouted Adamus. "Look at Man's art, look at his books, look at his poetry, his films, his television, his advertising—Love, Love, Love, that is all Man ever talked about, thought about, dreamed about, worked for—Man's whole time was spent in Love, except for a few necessary corrective wars, and even they were a direct outcome of Love."

All the members of the Board were looking at Logimus with incredulity.

"Well I'm sorry," he said defiantly, "but it seems to be a little unnecessary ..."

"Are you pursuing this obscene point?" demanded

27

Adamus, his ears twitching now, because his whiskers were so tangled they couldn't.

"Well, yes," said Logimus. "You see, the notion that God is Love . . ."

"Silence!" shouted Adamus. "The notion that God is Love is inviolable. God is Love! God is Love! God is Love! And it follows that Love is God."

"Hear, hear," said the Board. "God is Love and Love is God!"

Logimus shrugged, but said no more. There seemed little point.

"Thank you," said Adamus heavily, when he was convinced that Logimus had at last been silenced. "Now. Let's get on with this war."

6

The First Valley War was a rather higgledy-piggledy affair. The War Office, which was only the Board under another name, appointed two captains, Sinistermus and Dextermus, and told them to each pick a side of half a million male mice over the age of six weeks. Once the two armies were assembled they were marched to opposite ends of the Valley, and each mouse was issued with a sword and haversack containing three days rations. Outside broadcast vans travelled with each army so that the civilians could watch the war on their television sets.

"Now the theory of this, gentlemice," said Adamus, in the War Office, "is that this one battle should reduce our population of around three million by at least half a million."

Sinistermus and Dextermus both came through on the radio-telephone to report that their armies were ready.

"Good," said Adamus. "Well done."

"What do we do now?" asked Sinistermus.

"One of you launches a charge and you then have at each other with your swords."

"Righto," said Sinistermus.

"Roger," said Dextermus.

"Shall I launch the charge, or should you?" asked Sinistermus over the radio-telephone to Dextermus.

"You do it, old mouse," said Dextermus courteously.

So Sinistermus climbed up onto a little hill and looked down on his serried ranks of half a million mice,

all standing rigidly to attention with their swords at the salute.

"Mice!" he shouted. "We are about to attack the enemy. On the command 'charge' you will move forward at the double, maintaining formation, and on making contact with the enemy you will have at him with your swords."

"Hurray!" cheered the mice, waving their swords.

Sinistermus moved to the front of his troops and cried, "One. Two. Three. Charge!"

A great cry arose from the army as it moved forward as one mouse, rank upon rank, like a wave-crest rolling down the Valley.

Pleasantly conscious that he was leading the first mouse-charge in history, Sinistermus sprinted at the head of his columns.

"Charge!" he cried again in his enthusiasm.

The mice kept on charging, and charging, and charging.

"Charge!" cried Sinistermus once more, but a shade doubtfully because he had just realised that everyone had overlooked the fact that the enemy was at the other end of the Valley, by then still six kilometres away, and it takes a mouse a long time to charge that distance.

Sinistermus kept on shouting "Charge!" but after a couple of hours he was gasping for breath and not many of his followers could hear him.

By mid-day the mice were losing formation and many of them were limping badly, but still the enemy was not in sight. It was then that Sinistermus showed that he had the makings of a great general.

He turned to face his mice and held up his paw.

"Halt!" he cried. "We will now suspend the charge for lunch."

With grateful sighs the mice sat down and opened their haversacks.

In the War Office, Adamus looked worriedly at the television screen showing half a million mice munching sandwiches and opening bottles.

"I think this is rather irregular," he said.

After lunch Sinistermus made sure his troops tidied up their scraps and left no broken bottles on the ground, and then, at a rather more leisurely pace than before, began the charge again.

It was almost night-time when Sinistermus first sighted the banners of the Army of the Right. His mice were exhausted, and Sinistermus wondered whether it wouldn't be a good idea to camp for the night before going on with the bit about having at the enemy. But then he saw Dextermus leading his columns out to do battle and decided to get on with it.

The field of battle was a flat plain. The Armies of the Right and Left flowed across it towards each other, with enthusiastic cries on the one hand and tired squeaks on the other.

Dextermus and Sinistermus, as befitted their position, were well to the fore and were the first to meet in the centre of the plain.

"Hello, old mouse," said Dextermus. "My. You do look done in."

"Yes," said Sinistermus. "You can do the charging next time."

"Oh well," said Dextermus, looking a little uncertain, "what do we do now?"

"Have at each other I suppose," said Sinistermus.

"Yes, well," said Dextermus, raising his sword diffidently, "have at you."

"Have at you," said Sinistermus, tiredly raising his sword.

The mouse armies had stopped when their leaders met and were watching for some indication of what to do next. Most of the Army of the Left had sunk to the ground, panting.

Dextermus gave a tentative poke at Sinistermus's belly. Sinistermus moved aside and gave a swipe in the air over Dextermus's head.

"Do you think that'll do?" said Dextermus. "You do look rather tired."

"No, no," said Sinistermus. "I'm quite all right. We have to set an example for the mice after all."

He moved a little closer to Dextermus and took a cut at his legs.

Dextermus jumped in the air to avoid the blade and as he came down stumbled and twisted his ankle. He fell full-length on the ground.

"Oh, I say," said Sinistermus, "are you all right?"

"No. I've hurt my ankle," said Dextermus testily, "Give me a paw will you?"

Sinistermus switched his sword to his left paw and leaned forward to haul Dextermus to his feet. Dextermus, still clutching his own sword, came up slowly and tried his weight on his injured ankle.

"Ouch!" he squeaked, and stumbled forward, thrusting out his paws to break his fall.

Unfortunately he had forgotten that his right paw still held his sword, and as he straightened his arm he jerked the sword forward.

It went straight through Sinistermus's furry chest, through his lungs, through his heart, and out through his furry back.

Sinistermus sat down and died.

Back in the War Office the Board, who had been watching the progress of the first battle of the mice with some concern, broke into cheers. Their plan was beginning to work.

"Only another 499,999 casualties and our objective will have been achieved," said Sciemus gleefully.

The others all patted each other on the back and shook paws with each other. All except Logimus, who was looking at the television screen which still held the twitching body of Sinistermus. "I wonder, did it hurt?" he thought.

Meanwhile, Dextermus had limped back to the radio-telephone and got through to the War Office.

"There's been an accident," he said. "I suppose you saw it. What do you think I ought to do?"

"Nonsense," cried Adamus. "You've struck a great blow for the Right. Tell your men to go and do the same thing to all those rotten Leftists."

Up until this moment the Board had not been sure whether they ought to favour victory for the Left or the Right, and had finally decided that the only thing to do was to wait until the battle had been won and then be in favour of the victor, but now that the leader of the Left had been slain it seemed appropriate to favour the Right. The Board all murmured its agreement with Adamus's instructions.

Obediently, Dextermus carried out his orders.

"Go and stick your swords through all those rotten Leftists," he cried to the Army of the Right.

Equally obediently, the Army of the Right moved forward and stuck its swords into the bodies of the Army of the Left, who were so tired and surprised that mostly they just sat there and let the swords be stuck in. A few dozen fought back in a vague sort of way, but they were so discouraged that they were soon overcome and killed too. Several thousand saw what was happening and simply scampered away.

"Look at those cowards," said Sciemus disgustedly. "There ought to be some sort of penalty for that sort of thing."

"Hear, Hear!" said the Board.

"I suspect they ought to be given a medal," murmured Logimus, but everybody ignored him.

Very soon the plain was littered with the bodies of dead mice, mostly lying on their backs with swords stuck through their chests.

"I think, gentlemice," said Adamus, "it's time to call for a little champagne. The Right has won a great victory."

"We're still several thousand short of our objective," said Sciemus tentatively. "Do you think we could get some of the Right to fall on their own swords?"

"Come, come, Sciemus," said Adamus, "you mustn't be a perfectionist. This is only our first battle and I regard it as a great success. We'll do better next time and we can have a battle once a week if we want to."

His voice took on more sonorous tones as he accepted a glass of champagne from a steward.

"I think we can safely say the population problem has been solved, gentlemice," he said. "I would like to propose a toast to the infallibility of the Word of Man."

"To the Word of Man," intoned all the other members of the Board.

36

7

After that wars became a weekly affair in the Valley, but none was ever as successful as the first from the point of view of the Board. For one thing many mice, having seen the battle on television, became very reluctant to join either the Right or the Left, and the Board found it hard to organise armies of sufficient size to make the carnage worthwhile.

Adamus went off and studied and soon came up with an answer to that one.

"It's quite simple," he said to the Board. "We introduce conscription."

"What does that mean?" asked Sciemus.

"It means that every mouse we tell to

go into the army has to go into the army by law."

"And what if he won't?" asked Logimus.

"Then he goes to gaol."

"But surely that would be interfering with the rights of mice," said Logimus.

"Not at all," said Adamus. "Any rotter who won't do what his country wants him to do deserves to go to gaol."

"Did Man do that?" asked Logimus.

"All the time," said Adamus, triumphantly. "So that proves it right."

Logimus pondered for a moment, his brow furrowed as much as a mouse's brow can furrow.

"But didn't any Men prefer to go to gaol rather than go out and kill people?"

"Some did," admitted Adamus, "but on the whole Men preferred to do just about anything rather than go to gaol, and I'm sure mice will feel the same."

Adamus was right. A few dissident mice did refuse to be conscripted and were taken off to gaol, but not too many. Most thought the shame too great and preferred to take their chances in the Armies of the Right or Left. In fact those that did go to gaol weren't greatly incommoded because the cells had been built for human beings and most of the mouse prisoners slipped quietly through the bars and went home. A few strong-minded mice stayed in gaol and went on hunger strikes, but that didn't upset the Board. It just waited until the mice starved to death or got tired of it all and went home.

The second great problem the Board faced was that the mouse soldiers became too good. Once they knew they had to go into the army and take part in battles they soon realised that they had a much better chance of survival if they became competent soldiers. Night and day the mouse recruits trained with swords and shields; practising fencing, feinting, attack and counter-attack, methods of withdrawal, massed charges, tactical retreats and wars of attrition.

The result was that the tenth great battle between the Right and Left only produced about a thousand casualties, even though a million mice were engaged on either side. Adamus pushed a motion through the Board which brought about the formation of what he called a Third Force whose function, as he explained it, was to join any battle that was going and tear into both sides simultaneously. At first the confusion brought about by this manoeuvre increased the casualty rate substantially. However, most of these casualties were among the Third Force, with whom both the Right and Left became extremely, although perhaps illogically, annoyed. A few battles later the Third Force had become just as circumspect as the Right and Left and the casualty rate dropped alarmingly.

The population of the Valley reached twelve million. Even with these numbers the standard of living was not greatly affected. The streets were crowded, but the mice were still able to move provided they didn't mind being bumped and jostled every centimetre or so. There was food enough to go round, but there were always long queues outside the food stores, simply because there weren't enough stores for the number of mice demanding to be served. Unemployment became a problem. Given their state of technological advancement, the mice could produce all they needed with a relatively small workforce. They found, with a population of twelve million, that two million mice could easily produce all that was needed, and the rest had to go on the dole. This made recruiting for the Armies of the

Right and Left much easier and eventually the Board decided to stop conscription. The stage was even reached when the Army of the Left had two million troops and the Army of the Right had three million—right handed mice being more numerous—and the Board had to declare that no more recruits would be taken for the time being.

"Mice of the Valley!" Adamus cried in a television broadcast one night. "Unless you show the proper fighting spirit, the Valley will be in grave danger. We can't keep soldiers permanently employed unless they are actively engaged. There must be more casualties in our battles. I implore you. I beseech you. I order you. Mice of the Right and mice of the Left—get out there on the battlefield and do your duty, in the name of God, in the name of Love."

But all the mice did was become better and better soldiers, so that fewer and fewer were killed. It seemed that the mice were singularly reluctant to die.

"Do you think," asked Adamus at a Board meeting, "that there might be any point in an old suggestion of Logimus's that we should advocate mass suicide?"

Sciemus, Fawsmus and Mogimus looked uncertainly at each other.

"I wasn't altogether serious at the time," said Logimus.

"No. But do you think there might be something in it?"

"I think you'd have to make it compulsory," said Sciemus.

"And what penalties were you thinking of imposing on those who refuse," asked Logimus pointedly.

"Well," said Adamus tentatively, "Men did have a thing they called execution. We could issue a proclamation saying that any mouse who didn't commit suicide would be executed."

"Hey," said Sciemus, "that's not bad. What do you think, fellows?"

Mogimus and Fawsmus looked brighter than they had for some weeks.

"I think there might be something in it," said Fawsmus.

"It's neat," said Mogimus. "If they don't commit suicide they get executed. Either way the problem's solved; the population has to drop."

All the members of the Board except Logimus began to smile appreciatively, and the worry lines that had recently been developing on their faces began to smooth away.

"Well," said Adamus, "if we're agreed, let's make it a law and I'll issue a proclamation tonight. What do you say—all mice with tails more than nine centimetres long have to commit suicide under pain of execution. That should get rid of about two million or so."

The members of the Board, to a mouse, all turned and studied the length of their own tails.

"Naturally," said Adamus hastily, "there would be certain exceptions to the law."

"Do you think that would be fair?" asked Logimus.

"Of course it would be fair," said Adamus. "Somebody has to keep the Valley running. Are we agreed then?"

The Board all began to nod, but then Logimus, who had been fiddling with his slide-rule, stood up.

"Gentlemice," he said. "No sane mouse will obey this law."

"Then they'll all be executed," said Adamus impatiently.

42

Logimus sighed. "If you had a thousand executioners—and I doubt whether you'd find a quarter that number willing to do the job—working full-time, and if all the mice agreed to be executed without making a fuss, which I doubt very much, and if you had efficient execution equipment, which you haven't, you wouldn't affect the law of exponential growth by more than one quarter of one per cent. The idea is ludicrous."

The Board members looked dashed, but they knew better these days than to argue with Logimus on matters of mathematics.

"Oh well," said Adamus. "It was just an idea. Back to the drawing-board."

8

It was while browsing through an old copy of the New York Times that Adamus hit upon his next idea. He leaped to the telephone in great excitement and convened an extraordinary meeting of the Board at his home. It wasn't exactly his home by this stage, because he was sharing it with several thousand other mice, but he still had a reasonably sized section of one room partitioned off where he could conduct affairs of state.

Evemus, now grown rather portly in her middle age, and pregnant again, served tea and scones to the Board members, helped by her eldest daughter, who was also pregnant.

OUR BELOVED
CHAIRMOUSE

Adamus, the other members of the Board would have thought if they had been familiar with the simile, was looking like a cat who has just had a surfeit of cream. He wriggled impatiently on his seat, waiting for everybody to settle down. "Gentlemice!" he said at last. "I have the solution!"

The others looked at him intently and respectfully, although in their tiny hearts they doubted. They had heard too many solutions by this stage.

"As you know," said Adamus, "we have long been aware that Man made great use of the motor car during his days on earth, and we have in our deliberations often considered whether or not we should do the same."

The others nodded patiently.

"Always," said Adamus, who, to the worry of his colleagues, had developed a tendency to loquaciousness, "we came to the conclusion that our circumstances were different; that the distances in the Valley did not require the utilisation of the motor car."

"True, true," mumbled the Board members politely.

"Gentlemice," Adamus paused and looked each mouse steadily in the eye. This took him quite a while and Logimus had to stifle a yawn as he waited for the next word.

"Gentlemice," said Adamus. "We were wrong!"

He gazed triumphantly at the bemused faces of the Board.

"Wrong?" said Logimus at last, politely.

"Wrong!" said Adamus heavily.

"Why?" said Logimus.

"Because," said Adamus, "we completely misunderstood the purpose of the motor car for Man."

"But surely it was simply to carry people about?" said

47

Logimus.

"Not at all," said Adamus, pleased that he was to confound Logimus for once. "The motor car was a means of population control."

At this point he stood up and took hold of the New York Times, which had been reduced in size by a special process the mice had developed.

"According to the New York Times, no lesser authority than the New York Times," said Adamus, "the motor car killed more people than war ever did."

"Did it really?" said Logimus.

Adamus flourished the Times.

"Many, many more," he said. "In every country of the world, from the time it was invented, the motor car killed thousands upon thousands of people each year. You see it was working all the time, night and day, week in and week out, year after year, ceaselessly running over people."

"Did they do it on purpose, do you think?" asked Logimus who, as usual, was beginning to look puzzled.

"Of course they did," said Adamus. "Do you think Man would have gone on with the motor car, killing finally millions upon millions of people, if he hadn't been doing it on purpose?"

"And you think it was a means of population control?" said Logimus, still doubtful.

"Of course," said Adamus, who was beginning to be impatient with Logimus. "What else could it have been?"

"Of course," interjected Sciemus, rattling his teacup in excitement, "and not only that, but think of the injured . . . there must have been millions and millions who were injured too."

"So what?" said Adamus.

"Well," said Sciemus, "if they're lying in bed, maimed, they can't make Love can they?"

"By George," said Adamus, "you're right. I hadn't thought of that. Goodness, Man was ingenious wasn't he? Just by inventing the motor car he not only had transport but also rid himself of millions of surplus people and stopped millions more from procreating. Ingenious."

Logimus rattled his teacup irritably.

"Look," he said, "when I raised the point that we had a copulation problem rather than a population problem you all jumped on my neck. Now you intend to put half the population in hospital just so they can't make Love. What's the difference?"

Adamus looked amusedly superior.

"You don't understand," he said. "What we'll be doing by introducing the motor car is reducing the population. As a side effect of that we'll put a lot of mice in hospital. As a side effect of that they won't be able to copulate. Well, not much anyhow. But that's not what we intend. All we intend to do is reduce the population. All other results are accidental. If they happen to be beneficial, it's irrelevant."

Adamus, very proud of his incursion into philosophy, looked around at the Board who, except for Logimus, hadn't understood a word.

"That," he added, to settle the matter once and for all, "is called the principle of double effect."

"Oh," said the Board doubtfully.

"But . . ." began Logimus.

"But nothing," hurriedly interjected Adamus, who

wasn't all that keen on defending his argument. "The fact is Man had the motor car, so it must be good, and a combination of war and the motor car should play merry hell with the population problem. So let's get on with giving the Valley the inestimable benefit of the motor car."

"Hear, hear!" cried the Board members, and jiggled their teacups because there wasn't a table to thump.

The first motor car produced in the Valley was a mouse-sized version of an old style touring car. It was very big, relatively speaking, and had a V12 engine which gave it tremendous power. There had been some debate about whether to produce big or small cars. The advocates of the big car had won the day by arguing that, the bigger and more powerful the motor car, the more mice it could kill and maim. Those who favoured small cars could only produce some confused arguments about fuel economy, which really didn't seem to apply because the Valley had apparently limitless supplies of fuel in the old service stations.

The first car rolled off the assembly line, black and shining, to the cheers of the members of the Board, their wives and the factory workers. The manager of the works ceremonially handed the keys to Adamus. With courtly grace Adamus opened the off-side door and ushered Evemus in. Then he strode proudly around to the driver's side and climbed in himself.

"I say," said Logimus, nervously, "you're not going to drive it are you?"

"Of course," said Adamus airily, and stuck the key in the ignition.

"But do you know how?" said Logimus.

"Of course," said Adamus. "I've read the instruction book." He turned the key.

The engine roared enthusiastically and the car leaped forward, hitting fifty kilometres an hour before it reached the entrance to the works, which was fortunately open. It shot out, reducing the population by ten factory workers as it went.

"Goodness," said Mogimus, as he surveyed the twitching and broken bodies. "It does seem effective, doesn't it."

Adamus, finding his paws slightly ill-adapted to handling a steering wheel, hung on as best he could and managed to turn the huge machine into the thick flow of pedestrian traffic in the street outside.

By this stage there were so many mice in the Valley that they had to walk in step when they were outside, to avoid tripping over each other. All their tails stood upright in the air, held in place by a special harness designed to keep them that way so they wouldn't be constantly trodden on. These measures had made the movement of pedestrians just possible, but they were distinctly hampering when it came to trying to get out of the way of a speeding motor car.

Slightly horrified, despite himself, by what was happening, Adamus tried to put his foot on the brake, but only succeeded in stepping on the accelerator. It was estimated later that the car was travelling at eighty kilometres an hour when it hit the first pedestrians. The squeals of pain, fear and horror from thousands of tiny throats drowned the roar of the engine.

Nobody ever found out what the initial tally of the motor car was because most of the bodies were too squashed to be distinguished from one another, but the car went about fifty metres into the crowd before it was stopped by the marsh of blood and bone that it had created. Something like twenty kilograms of mashed mouse was carted off to the crematorium. There were 710 distinguishable dead bodies, and 986 severely crippled mice.

Startled by the incident, Evemus prematurely gave birth to ten babies, but this did not detract from the car's obvious potency as a population controller.

"Just think," said Adamus gleefully, as he and the other Board members waited around while the car was hosed down. "Just think—that was achieved when the

motor car was in the hands of an inexperienced driver and in just a matter of seconds. Imagine what a really good driver dashing about all day could manage."

"Indeed, indeed," said Adamus, rubbing his paws together. "I think, gentlemice, we can safely say that the population problem has been solved."

"Thanks to you, Mr Chairmouse," said Sciemus.

"Not me," said Adamus piously, "thanks to the Word of Man. Oh look," he added as the last of the blood and fur and little bits of bone were washed from the car's bonnet. "It's not damaged at all."

Adamus was so pleased by the success of this excursion into population control that he had himself crowned King on the strength of it. He had reached the letter 'S' in the Encyclopaedia Britannica and he was much struck by the article on 'Sovereigns'. But his crown wasn't comfortable and was too heavy to wear often, so he soon went back to being plain Chairmouse again.

The cars rolled off the production line at the rate of 1,000 a day and were issued to anyone who wanted them. There was no shortage of takers because as more and more cars took to the road it became obvious that the best chance of survival lay in being in one. As none of the mice could drive when they first started, the carnage was very impressive. Several houses had to be cleared of occupants and turned into hospitals, and the crematoria fires blazed night and day. Special dampeners had to be invented and fitted to the chimneys of the crematoria when the smell of cooking mouse began to pervade the Valley.

The screech of tyres and the blare of horns, mingled with the squeals of the dying and the crippled, became something of a nuisance but, as Adamus remarked, "You can't make an omelette without breaking eggs." This rather puzzled the rest of the Board, but it got the general drift.

Sciemus ingeniously reduced the noise level by having the horns removed from all the cars.

"After all," he said, "the purpose of the horn is to give warning of danger, and that's not at all what we want, is it?"

Sciemus received so much applause for this idea from

the other Board members that he went off and thought hard until he had another idea, then came back and recommended to the Board that cars should be manufactured without brakes. This was tried out on a batch of 100 cars and they were all wrecked within a matter of hours. Sciemus argued rather forlornly that at least the drivers of most of them had been killed, but even he found his position a little weak, in view of the vast numbers of deaths a car could produce if it kept going.

On Adamus's insistence the wars were maintained, even though the motor cars produced more deaths.

"After all," he said, "every little helps."

Curiously enough the wars became more popular with the advent of the motor car, simply because the battlefields were so much safer than the streets.

The members of the Board looked forward eagerly to the next census so they could see just how effective was their latest blow against over-population.

On census day they organised a modest book among themselves on what the new population figures would be.

"I'll bet on ten per cent lower than the last," said Adamus.

"I'll take twenty-five per cent lower," said Sciemus.

"I suspect that's a little optimistic," said Mogimus. "I'll settle for twenty."

"Fifteen," said Fawsmus.

They all looked at Logimus, whom they still respected in matters mathematical.

"What about you, Logimus?" said Adamus.

Logimus looked thoughtfully around at the Board members.

"I think it will be just under sixty million," he said

slowly.

"What?" squeaked Adamus.

"Nonsense," squeaked the other three members of the Board.

"Sixty million," said Logimus, "or rather, just under. It is just one year since I first brought to your attention the exponential law of growth and decay. On the figures that were available then the population was eleven thousand. I explained to you that one year later the population would inevitably be sixty million, unless something was done."

"But we did do something," squeaked Adamus. "The wars, the motor cars . . ."

"A few million deaths don't affect a progression of that sort very much," said Logimus. "As I said, I expect the total to be just under sixty million."

"But millions of mice have died," said Adamus.

"If ten million mice had died," said Logimus inexorably, "the total population would still be just under sixty million."

"But where could they all be?" said Adamus. "I mean, you drive out into the streets and into the fields, you don't see these vast numbers of mice."

"Of course not," snapped Logimus. "They are all inside, standing on one anothers' heads, virtually, to keep away from your wretched motor cars."

Adamus looked at him blankly.

"Are you sure about all this?" he said.

"No," said Logimus frankly, "but I see no reason to suppose my mathematics is wrong, so I'm betting on almost sixty million as the next census figure."

In the event, nobody found out exactly because the census taking broke down when the figure reached fifty million. The officials engaged in the counting realised that the population was leaping upwards before their eyes. They would start at one house in which they estimated perhaps a hundred thousand mice lived, and they would find that by the time they had gone through half the house there had been so many births amongst the mice already counted that the tally was already hopelessly wrong. So they would start again at the beginning, with exactly the same result.

"They're being born faster than we can count them," reported the head census taker, his little eyes red with fatigue, as he presented his figures to the Board.

"But what does it mean?" asked Adamus, in considerable dismay.

"It means," said Logimus, "that the population of the

58

Valley has reached saturation point. From now on, unless the death-rate equals the birth-rate, the Valley is doomed."

"But nothing we do seems to help," said Sciemus.

Adamus, badly shaken, sunk his chin onto his paws.

"I will again consult the Word of Man," he said, but without a great deal of conviction.

The best Adamus could come up with was to issue the whole population with copious supplies of alcohol and cigarettes, and make the consumption of both compulsory.

"I don't think they'll do much good," he told the Board apologetically, "but alcohol and cigarettes were certainly one of Man's population controls."

"But are they lethal?" asked Logimus.

"Oh they're lethal all right," said Adamus, "but it's very puzzling because they seem a bit slow. Far too slow for our problem I'm afraid."

"How do they work exactly?" asked Sciemus.

Adamus twitched his nose doubtfully.

"As far as I can make out," he said, "they're a sort of pleasant poison. You enjoy smoking and drinking the things that kill you in the end. But, as I said, they take too long. The alcohol seems to help make the motor car more efficient as a control, but really I must confess that I don't think either is the answer. They'll help, but we need something more."

"Did Man make cigarettes and alcohol compulsory?" asked Sciemus.

"He used a sort of psychological compulsion which he called advertising," said Adamus, "which worked very well, but I don't think we need bother. My guess is that the new controls will be very popular."

They were too. Before long the raucous squeaks from riotous drinking parties vied with the roar of motors and the shrieks of the injured. The mice took to free alcohol like ducks to water, and the medical mice soon began to discover encouraging signs of liver damage and wet brain. But, as Adamus had realised, it wasn't quick enough. It had the unfortunate side-effect of slowing down production at the automobile factory because the drunken workers found it difficult to assemble the complicated machinery, but this was almost compensated for by the increased death-rate on the roads.

"You see," Adamus told his Board, "it's quite obvious that Man used a number of population controls simultaneously. We have war and the motor car, cigarettes

and alcohol, and a nice level of pollution from the factories and the crematoria. With any luck soon, just in the natural course of things, we'll have starvation and disease, and in another year we'll move into the area where natural death will take a hand. But, as Logimus will so readily point out, it just isn't enough. The birth-rate is still going to be higher than the death-rate."

The Board members, all now aged beyond their years with the burden of office, sat gloomily around the Board table. They were all much more mellow and tolerant than when they began the task of controlling the Valley and Logimus wondered whether his point of copulation control might again be raised.

"Do you think," he began tentatively, "that it's possible our thinking might have been wrong all along . . . that . . ."

Adamus raised his head wearily.

"No, Logimus," he said gently. "I know what you're going to say, but we must keep the faith. God is Love."

"God is Love and Love is God," murmured the other Board members absently.

Logimus gave up.

"But there is a way," said Adamus. "Man *must* have had some other method or methods." He said this very firmly, with great conviction, and there was a stirring among the Board members of something akin to optimism. Then he spoilt the effect by adding plaintively, "Mustn't he?"

The Board members' heads sunk down on their paws.

And then Adamus discovered abortion.

"Whoopee!" he squealed, as he grasped the implications of an article he happened to come across while browsing through the Encyclopaedia Britannica. "Whoopee! This is it!"

It was a new, vibrant Adamus that faced the hastily convened Board meeting that day.

"Don't you see," he said, banging the table with his paw for emphasis, "if we make abortion automatically compulsory the population has to stay exactly where it is. If the population is stable all we need do is stand back and wait while the motor car, the wars and all the rest do their work and we'll actually have a decline in population. It's brilliant. Man always had the

62

answer."

"But Mr Chairmouse," said Logimus, "wouldn't it be just as easy not to . . ."

"Shut up Logimus," said Adamus cheerfully. "Don't go bringing up all that stale claptrap. This is the solution."

"But Mr Chairmouse," said Logimus, "you'll have to have millions of abortionists and millions of hospital beds devoted to nothing else."

"So? It helps solve the unemployment problem. Any more objections, Logimus?" asked Adamus triumphantly.

Logimus sat back in his chair. He knew that when the Chairmouse had discovered a new solution there was no stopping him and anyway, mathematically, there was some strength in this idea. He began fiddling with his slide-rule and Adamus eyed him nervously. Adamus always felt nervous when he saw Logimus fiddle with his slide-rule.

"Well, Logimus," he said. "Any more objections?"

"Just a minute please, Mr Chairmouse," said Logimus, and scribbled a few figures on a scrap of paper.

"But it has to be right," said Sciemus plaintively. "If every pregnant mouse has an abortion it stands to reason there can't be an increase in the population."

"Quite, quite," murmured Logimus, and kept on scribbling.

"Is it difficult to perform an abortion?" asked Fawsmus.

"No. No," said Adamus. "Just a couple of scrapes or a squirt or cut or two and it's all done."

"Mr Chairmouse," said Logimus. "It would take at least a month to get this scheme of yours into full operation."

"Yes, well?" said Adamus.

"By then the population will be well above the number the Valley can support, and starvation will be rampant."

"Yes, well. I can't help that, can I?" said Adamus.

"No. I just thought I'd point out the situation to you. The other thing is that if you succeed in achieving a nil birth-rate in exactly two years time there won't be a mouse alive in the Valley who isn't distinctly middle-aged, and most of them will be very elderly."

"Oh. Really?" said Adamus. "Yes. I suppose you're right. Still, will that matter?"

"You'll find it very hard to gather together a work-force capable of producing enough to keep the Valley going."

"Yes, yes," said Adamus testily, "but that's a problem that won't arise for a year or so will it?"

"No. But the starvation will."

"Well, that will only help control the population more, won't it," said Adamus.

"And weaken it," said Logimus.

"Oh well, you can't have everything," said Adamus. "In any case, something else will turn up. Obviously we haven't consulted all the works of Man yet. Just look at the progress we've made on population control since we started. Abortion is the obvious next big break-through and no doubt there'll be something in the works of Man to solve any other problems that arise. Are we all agreed, gentlemice?"

"Just a minute, Mr Chairmouse," said Logimus.

"Well, Logimus, what is it? I'm not prepared to listen indefinitely to carping criticism," said Adamus.

"Just a question, Mr Chairmouse. Do you propose to

have all the means of population control going simultaneously? I mean war, the motor car, alcohol, tobacco, pollution and abortion—keeping in mind that you'll soon have starvation and disease as well?"

"Yes," said Adamus firmly. "You can't have too much of a good thing. Besides, it's exactly what Man did."

This clinched the argument. The Board unanimously decided to launch Operation Abortion.

Establishing the abortion clinics was much easier than producing the motor car, the mice found. It was simpler to perform an abortion than assemble an internal combustion engine, and there was no difficulty in finding any number of mice willing to be trained as abortionists. Several dozen houses had to be cleared of occupants to provide room for the clinics, but there were so many mice already living in the fields by now that it didn't matter much.

Policing the new law provided no difficulties. It was simply assumed that any female mouse over three weeks old was pregnant and, unless she had a certificate saying she'd had an abortion the previous day, she was carted off to the clinic and given the treatment.

The major problem was the disposal of the embryos. Graveyards had long since been abandoned as too wasteful of space and the crematoria were working to capacity and still couldn't cope. The problem was partly solved by open air incineration, but this had unpleasant side effects, and finally vast refrigeration plants were installed to store the embryos until the crematoria could be extended.

Unfortunately Logimus's prediction proved true, and

the mice didn't manage to get the population increase to a nil level before the Valley went well into the starvation zone, but, as Adamus said, "At least we're making some progress."

9

Sciemus, who still remembered his brief moment of glory when he suggested removing horns from motor cars, took to spending a great deal of time in the School of Homological Studies, hoping to come across an idea which would attract the same degree of applause. He was somewhat tentative about his project because he hadn't forgotten his sense of failure over the scheme to remove brakes from motor cars. However, when he finally discovered his idea it was of such overwhelming magnitude that he didn't for one moment doubt that he would be hailed as a genius.

"I shall go down in history as the saviour of mousekind," he murmured to himself in awe, as he read and re-read the statistical findings of Man on what was apparently the ultimate population control.

"Megadeaths," he said to himself, rolling the word opulently around his tongue. "Megadeaths. What a lovely expression. This will make the motor car obsolete. Who ever heard of one motor car causing one megadeath, let alone a thousand?"

But when he raised the idea at the next Board meeting he was aggrieved to find that the other mice didn't leap to their feet with howls of applause.

"Well, I don't know," said Adamus slowly. "It doesn't sound the sort of thing we ought to rush into." In fact he was a little put out that Sciemus should have come up with what seemed to be a very good idea. Adamus felt that if the solution should ever be found it was he that should find it.

"But ... but ... megadeaths," muttered Sciemus plaintively, "megadeaths."

"Might be a bit hard to sell," said Mediamus cautiously.

"Mightn't they be beyond our technical resources?" asked Fawsmus.

"No," said Sciemus, who felt he was on sure ground here. "One was once made by a schoolboy it seems. All sorts of people had them!"

"Oh, really?" said Fawsmus. "That sounds all right then. Why not give a few to the Armies and let's see what happens?"

"Why not?" said Mogimus, who really didn't know what anybody was talking about.

Sciemus began to relax.

"I have all the relevant technical information here,"

he said, patting his briefcase. "There's no reason why we shouldn't go into production immediately, if everyone's agreed."

"Now just a moment," said Adamus, who was feeling distinctly nettled by now. "I said I don't think this is the sort of thing we should rush into. Did Man use these things?"

"Once or twice as a direct population control," said Sciemus, "but he was always letting them off and making bigger and better ones. Obviously he intended to use them or why would he have made them?"

"Hmm," said Adamus, baffled.

Logimus gave a sarcastic sniff.

"Ah," said Adamus, who felt that Logimus could always be called upon to throw cold water on any idea. "What do you think Logimus?"

Logimus's sniff had drawn two of his whiskers up one of his nostrils and it took him a few moments to get them out.

"Absolute bloody nonsense," he said at last.

Sciemus gaped.

"But ... megadeaths," he said. "Megadeaths!"

"It's no good squeaking 'megadeaths' as though it was a magic word. The whole point is that you'd have too many megadeaths."

"How can there be too many megadeaths?" said Sciemus.

"Just one of these things let off in the Valley would wipe out every living mouse," said Logimus sharply.

"Oh," said Sciemus lamely, "would it?"

"Yes," said Logimus, fiddling with his slide-rule. "Want me to prove it?"

"No, no," said Sciemus hastily. But because he was

reluctant to abandon his niche in history he added, "Wouldn't that solve the problem?"

The others looked at him pityingly, and he realised how foolish he was being. He slumped back in his chair and was heard from no more at the meeting, apart from an occasional sigh of 'megadeaths', as though he was mourning some lost vision of paradise.

Adamus, who was inclined to be generous now that Sciemus had been routed, said kindly, "Don't take it too much to heart, old mouse. It was a good try. I'll look into that area myself. There might be something in it that you've missed. As you said, obviously Man didn't make these things for nothing."

So Adamus devoted the next few weeks to finding out all he could about nuclear fission. He found it all very brain-bending, and for the life of him he could find nothing to disprove Logimus—even the most minute version of a nuclear explosion would eliminate every mouse in the Valley. He saw the point of course—Man had had a much greater area to work in and could afford to take out vast sections of population and still have enough space left for the remainder.

"Nevertheless," he said to Evemus one evening, "I can't help feeling there's something in this. You see Man didn't use nuclear explosions, at least not much, and yet he had this tremendous potential for population control at his fingertips. And the other thing is he kept on letting them off in areas where there was no population."

"It's very strange, dear," said Evemus absently.

"And he didn't use them for war—at least not as a general habit. Yet you'd think that these things in the

70

hands of armies would have been a superb population control—given that you had the space to use them in."

"Yes, dear," said Evemus.

"Of course," said Adamus, "there is the question of power, but I can't see that that helps us. Not with the population anyway."

"Well I don't know, of course, dear," said Evemus, "but it seems to me that there might be some point in cutting the average life-expectancy by half." She was absorbed in her knitting and was unaware of the startled look on Adamus's face.

"Eh?" he squeaked, making her drop a stitch.

"Eh what, dear?" said Evemus.

"What did you say?"

"What about?"

"About cutting the life-span by half."

"Oh, that," said Evemus, placidly resuming her knitting. "I just said it seems to me that there might be some point in cutting life-expectancy in half. I wouldn't know, of course. Maybe you'd better ask Logimus."

But Adamus didn't ask Logimus. Before the next meeting of the Board he brooded over his favourite work of Man, the New York Times. He was struck by a series of letters to the editor over a period of a year or two, near the End, just before the Beginning. He read them over and over again with growing excitement. There were letters from academics, students, mining magnates, and all sorts of people and they were all about one aspect of Sciemus's suggestion which had not previously struck him. Together with Evemus's remarks, the whole thing began to make sense.

Adamus dragged Evemus from her rocking-chair and

whirled her round and round. "We've found it, we've found it" he squeaked breathlessly.

"What?" panted Evemus, as she collided heavily with the rocking-chair.

Adamus stood still and collected himself. "You see, Evemus, it's the old principle of double effect rearing its head again," he puffed, regarding her earnestly. "Man wasn't using the bomb to control population at all, or at least not directly. It was just one effect of his real population check, sort of the icing on the cake. The real stuff was created before he even got to the bomb stage. Don't you see—it's not fallout they were on about, it was plutonium! Look at this editorial—Plutonium Economy! Apparently it reached the stage where some groups were even putting it in the water supply, like fluoride!"

"Why? Was it good for their teeth?" asked Evemus, who hadn't understood a word of this.

Adamus laughed indulgently. "I don't know about their teeth, but it just might be what we're looking for. Look dear, I won't be home for dinner—I've got to see Sciemus."

Evemus didn't bother telling him that there wasn't anything for dinner anyway. She smiled fondly and picked up her knitting again.

"It just about provides everything," Adamus shouted excitedly at the next meeting. "Leukaemia, cancer, sterility, natural abortion. Don't you see, Sciemus was almost right. The point he missed was that explosions were only the beginning of the method developed by man. Once you get this stuff into the atmosphere and the water supply you've got the solution. What about it Logimus? Would it cut life-expectancy by half?"

Logimus consulted his slide-rule.

"Yes," he said doubtfully, "accepting the facts as outlined in that editorial. But you've got a problem."

"Oh?" said Adamus, shaken. "What?"

"Well, to get a thing like this going you'd have to have a large and healthy workforce, and you just haven't got one any more, particularly not if you want to keep up the abortion clinics. I mean, at the moment almost a quarter of the population is fully engaged in abortion."

"Well, can't we cut that and concentrate on the other?"

"You can," said Logimus, "but you'll have a vast leap in the population."

"But then we will have a population with a life-expectancy of only eighteen months. Won't that even things out in the end?" said Adamus, who had acquired a smattering of mathematics.

Logimus looked doubtful.

"That's true in theory," he said, "but the principle of diminishing returns won't apply for about eighteen months, and in that time the population will go to something like double."

"But after that it'll be all right?"

"It could be. But it won't be tolerable in the meantime."

"But what if we had an all-out effort, double the war effort, produce twice the number of motor cars, treble the alcohol and cigarette rations. What if we all pulled together for one great heroic effort to keep the population down until this gets working. How about that?"

Logimus shook his head doubtfully.

73

"In theory," he said, "and purely mathematically, you could be right. But it seems to me that Man hadn't done all that much work on this latest method of population control, and it mightn't work out that way. I mean, he really didn't seem to know what the effect of this stuff would be."

"But," said Adamus triumphantly, "he did let it loose. Lots of times and in lots of places. He must have known what he was doing, and if we do the same how can we go wrong? What do you think, gentlemice?"

The other members of the Board knew that Adamus was going to get his own way whatever they said. They were too tired and hungry to think about it much anyway. The situation was going to be intolerable in the next eighteen months whatever happened, and there was always the outside chance that it might work. So they all bent their grizzled little heads and hammered out the requirements for Operation Uranium.

The operation was quite successful, up to a point. A week after the first dumping of wastes, strange and hideous diseases spontaneously developed. It was common to see mice dragging themselves through the streets under the weight of gigantic tumours. The death-rate soared spectacularly in the first weeks, but then evened out.

The abortion clinics found they were getting less work as females began to miscarry spontaneously. Then they usually died, which helped things along too. The clinics temporarily stopped operations, with the result that a number of the hardier females came to term. The mice they produced were pretty startling. Adamus's favourite great-great-great-great-great-granddaughter had a litter

of babies, each of which had two heads. They all died, but Adamus became uneasily aware as the weeks passed of a new phenomenon—new mutant mice everywhere who did not die, even though they had all sorts of things very conspicuously wrong with them. They lived in the fields and occasionally produced even more peculiar offspring, and they seemed impervious to higher levels of nuclear waste. It was all very worrying.

Adamus's other projects to increase smoking, drinking and driving never eventuated. All the mice were simply too ill and too tired to do anything much except lie around. Large numbers of them died daily, but Logimus was correct; it was going to take too long for any increase in the death-rate to make much impact on the population as it stood. There seemed nothing to do but wait for the end.

But for the uncounted millions of mice and mutant mice in the Valley the end was taking its time in coming. Life still went on, up to a point.

10

One day, a year later, Adamus sat on the part of the verandah allocated to himself and Evemus and gazed at the morning light on the pollution cloud that hung permanently over the Valley. He was now an old mouse, and a melancholy sense of his own mortality had settled upon him. He turned to Evemus, who was knitting a layette, although she hadn't given birth to a live mouse for twelve months. "You know, my dear," he said. "There must have been something else I could have done."

"No mouse could have done more for the Valley than you did, my dear," said Evemus soothingly. She had become accustomed to fits of depression in Adamus as he grew older.

"No. It's kind of you to say so, but if I'd been the mouse I should have been I would have found the solution."

"But surely you have. The population has stayed at eighty million for almost a year."

Adamus looked affectionately at his wife. For the past year she'd taken little active interest in affairs of state, and was content to run the house for him. Which was fair enough, he mused; she'd given birth to 240 children and had had twenty-eight abortions to date. It was reasonable that she should slow down a little.

"Yes," he said, "but the point, my dear, is that it hasn't worked out the way it ought to have."

"Mmm?" said Evemus.

"I mean, you remember what it was like at the Beginning, when there was just you and me. When we had a green and silent Valley and the whole world was ours?"

"Of course I do, dear," said Evemus, and reached a gnarled paw across to stroke Adamus's greying forehead.

78

"And now look at it—jam-packed with malformed drunken mice with cigarettes stuck in their mouths, racing around in screeching motor cars when they're not involved in the weekly war or taking time off to have an abortion. I mean, do you think it was meant to be like this?"

Evemus peered at him sympathetically through her spectacles.

"There, there, dear, there was nothing else you could have done. And it's worked. You've achieved population control."

Adamus shifted in his chair. He found his bones ached these days if he sat in the one place too long. It might have something to do with the mercury he'd had introduced into the Valley's water supply.

"Yes, my dear," he said, "but we achieved it too late. By the time we found the solution the population was too big—exactly, I must confess, as Logimus had predicted."

"Well," said Evemus brightly, "what happened to your idea of more wars, more motor cars, more tar content in the cigarettes, stronger alcohol—it shouldn't be hard."

"No, dear," said Adamus patiently, "you don't understand. You see once we entered the starvation zone, production per head dropped enormously. It's simple enough—everyone's too weak to work properly and less is being produced. We still have most of the very small workforce there is left engaged in Operation Abortion, and that makes things much worse. The fact is that almost every mouse alive today is in an advanced state of malnutrition."

"Well," pursued Evemus, anxious to be helpful, "why

not stop the abortions for a while and increase the work-force producing food?"

"Obviously, my dear," said Adamus, "because that would mean an immediate increase in the population, which would only make things very much worse."

Evemus puzzled over this for a moment.

"Yes, of course," she said finally. "It's a sort of vicious circle, isn't it?"

"Exactly," said Adamus. "And it's getting more vicious. We're soon going to have to allow some births just to provide workers young enough to be able to do anything. And there won't be enough food for them so they'll grow up weak and inefficient and won't be much use anyhow. No, my dear, I'm afraid that unless we come up with something soon civilisation in the Valley is going to break down completely."

"Oh well," said Evemus, "maybe that will give every-body a good shaking up and things will sort themselves out."

Adamus smiled indulgently.

"You should talk to Logimus about that. If civilis-ation breaks down, all that'll happen is that the popu-lation will increase wildly and the race will degenerate simultaneously. It's a hideous prospect."

"Oh dear," said Evemus. "You are depressed."

"I am a little," said Adamus. "I did all that a mouse could do. I gave our people all the benefits of Man's wisdom that I could, and it just hasn't been enough."

"Anyhow, dear," said Evemus, "you kept the faith."

"I did, I suppose," said Adamus musingly. "You'd think, given that, that everything would have worked out all right, wouldn't you? And just look at our Valley now." He stared bleakly out from the verandah at the vista of smoking chimneys from the hundred of crematoria, at the dismal bulks of the dozens of refrigeration plants holding the embryos awaiting cremation, at the crowded streets strewn with the bodies of the latest traffic victims and deep in broken whiskey bottles and cigarette butts. In the distance he could see the flashes and flares of the latest war (they had long since graduated to bombs and napalm, but these hadn't proved significantly more efficient than swords), and over to the west he could see the spires of the euthanasia centres. These had proved surprisingly popular in the past twelve months.

Adamus sighed.

"No, my dear," he said. "It is difficult to escape the conclusion that we blew it."

However, by lunch-time Adamus had cheered up a little and after a good bottle of wine—he was careful, where practical, to set a proper example to the mice of the Valley—he suddenly had an idea.

It was the first idea he'd had for about six months and it quite startled him at first.

"Goodness," he thought, as he turned the idea over and over in his mind, examining it from every possible angle. "Goodness. I wonder would that be heretical?"

He strode backwards and forwards in his dining-room, with Evemus regarding him anxiously over her knitting, and the idea grew and grew in his mind.

When it had reached the size where his brain would burst if he didn't do something about it, he put through a telephone call to Logimus.

"Logimus, old mouse," he said, "I wonder could you give me some advice?"

81

"Of course, Mr Chairmouse," said Logimus politely.

"Now, you know how we've built our civilisation on the Word of Man."

"Yes, Mr Chairmouse," said Logimus cautiously, fearing that something was coming.

"And everything we've ever done has been a faithful replica of what Man did?"

"Yes, Mr Chairmouse."

"Well, it hasn't really worked out, has it?"

Logimus didn't answer for a moment. The understatement was so wild that he wondered whether the Chairmouse was quite sober.

"You could say that, Mr Chairmouse."

"Well," said Adamus, "I've been wondering. Do you think the problem could be that we haven't gone far enough?"

Logimus thought about that.

"I don't quite see where you're heading Mr Chairmouse. I would say that we've applied the methods we've used to their fullest extent. The trouble is that they haven't worked."

"Precisely," said Adamus, triumphantly. "And do you know why?"

"No, Mr Chairmouse," said Logimus. "Frankly I don't."

"Did it ever cross your mind that it could possibly be because we've only done what Man did, and never what he *would have done*?"

"I'm not sure that I follow you, Mr Chairmouse."

"It's quite simple," said Adamus excitedly. "You see, we took over from Man when he still had many of the problems that we have."

"All of them, in fact, Mr Chairmouse," said Logimus.

"All right. All of them. Now he would have done something else if he had continued, would he not?"

"That seems possible, Mr Chairmouse," said Logimus, very cautiously.

"Then," said Adamus, concluding his case, "you see nothing wrong with my putting a proposition to the Board based on what Man would have done."

"Not in the least," said Logimus. By now he had a thoroughly agnostic attitude to anything that emanated from the works of Man.

"Thank you Logimus. In that case I would like you to round up the Board members and come to my home for dinner this evening."

"Dinner?" said Logimus, who hadn't been invited out to a meal for months. "I presume we should bring our own rations?"

"Not at all," said Adamus airily. "My treat."

He hung up, and a very puzzled Logimus set about

ringing up the members of the Board and inviting them to the Chairmouse's dinner.

The Board members and Logimus turned up promptly at seven. They were all very grey and a little bowed. They were also somewhat undernourished, despite the fact that they, as the Valley's administrators, had naturally had a better ration of food for the past year than the common mouse.

They trooped into the dining-room and were astonished to find that the table had been set for a formal dinner. A gleaming white table-cloth had been laid and each of the six places was carefully set with silver and a napkin. Candles on the table added to the graciousness of the occasion. Adamus welcomed his guests effusively and insisted they should have cocktails before dinner.

Each of the guests had a couple of drinks, but they talked little. They were acutely aware, by virtue of having been invited to a meal and the Chairmouse's obvious

excitement, that something big was afoot.

Adamus consulted his watch.

"Yes," he said. "Everything should be quite ready now. Please sit down, gentlemice."

The mice checked the name cards at each place and sat down, while Adamus struck a few notes on a gong on the sideboard.

Almost immediately the door of the dining-room swung open and in trooped six mousemaids. Each carried a covered silver dish from which seeped steam and the most delicious smells. It was clear that each dish contained a great deal of food; considerably more than the average monthly per capita ration.

The mousemaids laid the dishes just beside the diners and stood hovering, awaiting the order to serve.

"And now, gentlemice," said Adamus proudly, "let me present you with The Final Solution."

The mousemaids lifted the dishcovers.

Logimus screamed.
And screamed.